This book
belongs to:

Just imagine . . . growing, **flying**, sleep
blowing, **swimming**, eating, playing,
rollerskating, parent-frightening, **readi**
falling, **bird-riding**, washing, sailing, l
rusting, unravelling, **nibbling**, scarir
dinosaur-hunting, chariot-riding, chimn
demonstrating, fancy-dressing, **jousting**,
rumbling, **rolling**, grinding, clanging, pu
squeaking, huffing, **bubbling**, spell-ca
charming, rope-climbing, magic-carpet
brewing, **Pegasus-riding**, roaring, howl
chomping, leaping, **chewing**, splashing
buzzing, **snorting**, bounding, resting, t
scuttling, scurrying, **jumping**, walking
tunnelling, digging, fossil-hunting, **burro**
cycling, wheeling, **driving**, unicycling, m
riding, **helicopter-flying**, diving, floatin

y, sneezing, walking, **shouting**, chasing,
escuing, **shrinking**, writing, climbing,
, running, biting, drinking, **escaping**,
ning, transforming, **wobbling**, melting,
stretching, popping, time-travelling,
-sweeping, **spaceship-flying**, evacuating,
ing, Viking-meeting, **inventing**, whirring,
ng, buzzing, **creaking**, slurping, beeping,
ng, wish-granting, bewitching, **snake-**
ding, **fire-breathing**, egg-laying, potion-
, changing, hanging, racing, **crawling**,
swinging, **sliding**, slithering, laughing,
ting, munching, nibbling, **ball-chasing**,
feeding, cuddling, creeping, **exploring**,
ng, painting, treasure-hunting, **whizzing**,
rbiking, **hang-gliding**, hot-air ballooning,
gliding, sinking, discovering, dreaming,

For everyone who loves Heffers Children's Bookshop
– P.G.

For Lily, Lucy, Emily, Jessica, Florence and Henry
– N.S.

JUST IMAGINE
A PICTURE CORGI BOOK 978 0 552 56356 7

Published in Great Britain by Picture Corgi Books,
an imprint of Random House Children's Publishers UK
A Random House Group Company

Doubleday edition published 2012
This edition published 2013

3 5 7 9 10 8 6 4 2

RANDOM HOUSE CHILDREN'S PUBLISHERS UK
61–63 Uxbridge Road, London W5 5SA

www.randomhousechildrens.co.uk
www.randomhouse.co.uk

Addresses for companies within The Random House Group Limited can be found at:
www.randomhouse.co.uk/offices.htm
THE RANDOM HOUSE GROUP Limited Reg. No. 954009

A CIP catalogue record for this book is available from the British Library.

Printed in China

The Random House Group Limited supports the Forest Stewardship Council® (FSC®), the leading international
forest certification organisation. Our books carrying the FSC label are printed on FSC® certified paper. FSC is
the only forest certification scheme endorsed by the leading environmental organisations, including Greenpeace.
Our paper procurement policy can be found at www.randomhouse.co.uk/environment.

JUST IMAGINE

Imagine being as big as a house!

Or as tiny as a flea!

Take a look inside this book, and decide what you'd like to be.

Words by Pippa Goodhart   Pictures by Nick Sharratt

Picture Corgi

Can you imagine being BIG?

Or would you like to be small?

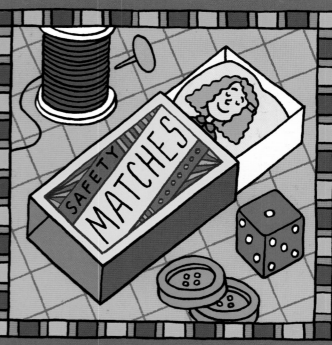

Imagine being made differently

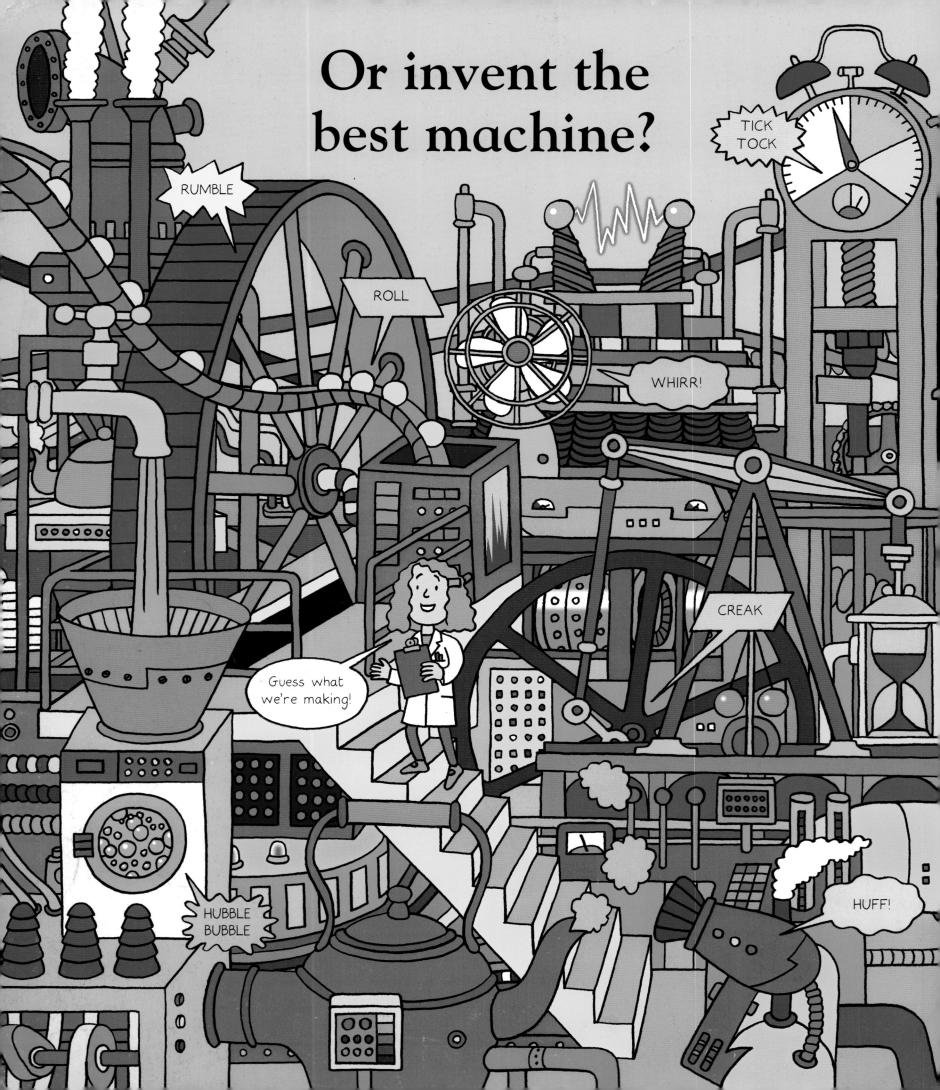

Imagine being magical

Imagine being an animal,

living in the wild.

Perhaps you'd rather be a pet, belonging to some child.

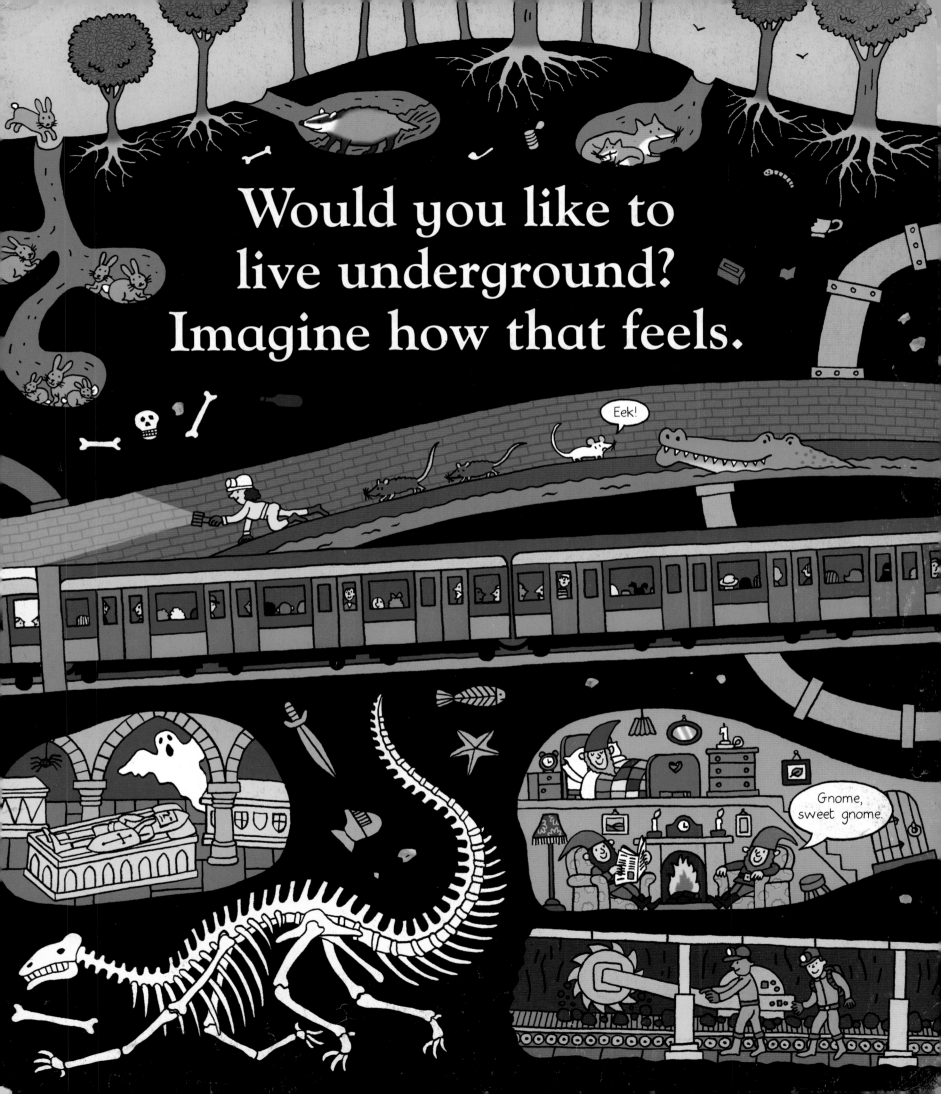

Or would you
like to whizz around
on some kind of wheels?

Close your eyes and dream yourself

Just imagine . . . growing, **flying**, sleep
blowing, **swimming**, eating, playing,
rollerskating, parent-frightening, **readi**
falling, **bird-riding**, washing, sailing, le
rusting, unravelling, **nibbling**, scarin
dinosaur-hunting, chariot-riding, chimn
demonstrating, fancy-dressing, **jousting**,
rumbling, **rolling**, grinding, clanging, pu
squeaking, huffing, **bubbling**, spell-ca
charming, rope-climbing, magic-carpet
brewing, **Pegasus-riding**, roaring, **howl'**
chomping, leaping, **chewing**, splashing
buzzing, **snorting**, bounding, resting, tr
scuttling, scurrying, **jumping**, walking
tunnelling, digging, fossil-hunting, **burro**
cycling, wheeling, **driving**, unicycling, mc
riding, **helicopter-flying**, diving, floatin

, sneezing, walking, **shouting**, chasing, escuing, **shrinking**, writing, climbing, , running, biting, drinking, **escaping**, ning, transforming, **wobbling**, melting, stretching, popping, time-travelling, sweeping, **spaceship-flying**, evacuating, ing, Viking-meeting, **inventing**, whirring, ng, buzzing, **creaking**, slurping, beeping, ng, wish-granting, bewitching, **snake-** ling, **fire-breathing**, egg-laying, potion- , changing, hanging, racing, **crawling**, swinging, **sliding**, slithering, laughing, ting, munching, nibbling, **ball-chasing**, feeding, cuddling, creeping, exploring, ng, painting, treasure-hunting, **whizzing**, rbiking, **hang-gliding**, hot-air ballooning, gliding, sinking, discovering, dreaming

Some more
unimaginably good books
illustrated by Nick Sharratt